The Snowflake

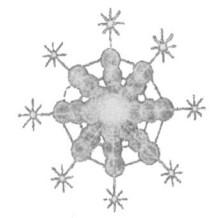

by

Robin Langford

Book Cover and Illustrations by Robin Langford

*This is dedicated to all
who love Christmas.*

The Snowflake

The Snowflake

One minute
Before Christmas
And high on a hill,
A star stood large
And perfectly still,
As moonbeams shone
From a dark satin sky
Spreading their beams
Onto shadows so high.
Everything was waiting
For the silent snow fall,
And nothing seemed to want
To move at all.
'Twas as if the night
Were holding its breath…
(Even the Owl
Delivered no death
As a mouse scuttled
Disturbing the peace
And then realised
T'would do better
To cease).

The air was crisp
And had a slight chill,
But behind it all
There was a huge thrill
For there was
Magic this night
And a wish to fulfill -
As was told in the book
The Legends of Old…

…All over the world
People looked
To the heavens,
Hoping that night
Good luck would be theirs,
And that they would be rich
And so would their heirs.

The Snowflake

Like the bold Mr. Gold
So gross and so fat
(His head was so big
There wasn't a size
He could wear for a hat)
Who bought a building
Where there nested a stork
(Which he soon moved on)
In the heart of New York -

He bought all the buildings
That rivaled its height
And banned all the planes
From flying that night -
(He banned them at least
From flying that way)
Just in case they blew
The Snowflake astray.

Or the Smedley-Smooth
In her London mews,
Who thought it a ruse
For her to use
Her maid called "Kitty,
Kitty Goodshoes,"
To stand on the balcony

Instead of her
Out in the cold for it
(Tho' wrapped in fake fur).
Not knowing that the maid
On catching the flake
Would wish lots of wishes
And off she would make,
Off over there
To a foreign clime
And never, never work
'Til the end of time.

Mr. Thin & Ms. Plain
(Known by some
As the Pin & Pain)
Had shown their cunning
With a huge great kite
Which they already
Had put in flight.
For it flew up high
From a church's steeple
Way above
The ordinary people,
So if the flake
Were to fall that way
It would catch it carefully
And they'd wish away -
(He'd be fat
And she'd be cute,
Tho' whether or not
It both would suit)
Together they sat
Gazing on high
Up to the stars
With a hopeful sigh.

There was
Mr. and Mrs.
Ha Pi Fat,
Whose son
Was called
La Zi Fat,
(For all
He seemed
To do all day
Was to sit and eat,
Not work or play).
They saw that when
They were old and grey
He'd still do nothing
Every day.
For many years
They had despaired
And in many ways
Their views had aired,
So when they heard
Of this wondrous tale -
In hope they sat
On a mountain top
That into their bowl
The flake would plop.

Even Ministers and Presidents
Around the world
Conspired, intrigued
And set their plans
To have the Snowflake
In their hands -
Using secret planes
And 'copters too,
Rockets and beams
To seize their dreams.

While,
Bishops and Priests
Nuns and Vicars
Knelt to pray
In their Sunday knickers,
Hoping that prayer
Would divert its motion
Towards their saintly
Churches and towers,
And give them spiritually
Unlimited powers.

News reporters
And 'telly' stations
Across the globe
Flashed revelations,
And had discussions
On this and that
And what would be
Its repercussions.

Astronomers with
Their big bug eyes
Looked through telescopes
And watched the skies
Searching for the magic flake
In the silent star filled lake,
Hoping to find
And upon it look
And then write it in
A hard-backed book.

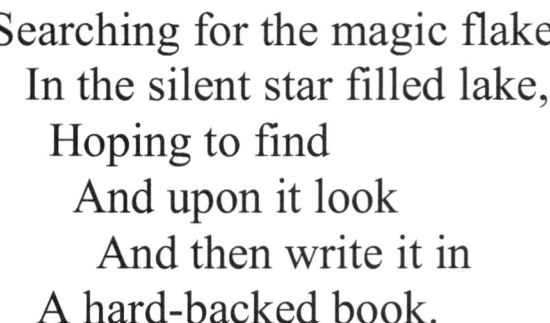

Witch doctors
In darkened huts
Muttered spells
For village chiefs,
While chieftain wives
Looked to the sky
With huge great
Leaves standing by
Ready to catch it
If it fell
And make their chieftains
Happy and swell.

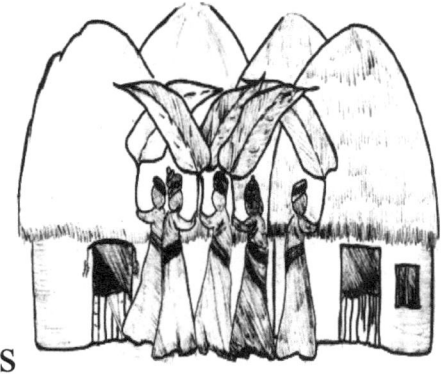

Artists also of various kinds
Meditated with their minds,
Whilst they sat
In dramatic positions
(Imagining making
Film decisions)
Compelling the flake
To fall their way
Through their Muse's
Hands that day.

The Snowflake

Kings and Queens
In marble halls
Sent commands
From castle walls,
That should any
In their kingdoms
Catch the flake
They would - a Prince
Or Princess make.

Lovers with their
Hands entwined,
Stood on hills
(Having wined
and dined)
And gazed at the moon
And wondered if
The flake would fall
As a gift,
So that they could love
For all of time
And then life would be
One happy rhyme.

Meanwhile,
In a village small,
A family was huddled
In their hall,
Round a hearth
Which was well fired,
Their faces tearful
And looking tired -

Except for one
(Who in the shadows
Appeared the smallest)
Called, "Little One Fallows."
Now, Little One she
Had shed no tears
For being little
She held no fears,
She'd heard the others
Sniff and cry
And was curious to know
What and why.
There was no reason
She could find
(But then she since birth
Had been born blind).

She'd listened carefully
To what they'd said -
They seemed to say
That her father was dead,
No news had come
From the Northern Sea
Where he'd been diving
For a generous fee -

But she in her darkness
A year to this day,
Remembered him saying
He'd be there and away,
Back to his loves,
Back to his treasures,
Back to his home,
And ne'er again roam.
He'd whispered those words
Deep, into her dreams
And said he was travelling
On a 'magical' stream.
Nightly she'd wished
On that heavenly stream
That it would bring him home, safe,
On its wonderful beams,

With arms open wide
And so much to say
And happiness through
That one Christmas Day.
These nightly wishes
Kept the darkness at bay,
For when she was frightened
The darkness would play,
It would be blacker than pitch
Thicker than thick,
She would feel nearly dead
Very ill and quite sick -
And now with these fears
From all of the others
The darkness grew thicker
And determined to smother.

But then she remembered
His promise to come home,
And that he'd never again,
Never leave them alone -
She knew he'd come through
On that "magical stream"
As his voice had said softly
To her in her dream.

But far away
In a cold dark sea,
(Where every evil
In a dream could be)
Her father was trapped,
And his knee was shattered,
And the whole of his body
Was brutally battered.
Some rope was tangled
Round a rock
And webbing,
And his life was
Very quickly ebbing,
Air was bubbling
Leaking and lacking
As his hold on life
Was easily slackening.
Once let go
He'd remain below
Never to rise
From the murkiness there
Up to the love
Which wanted to care.
To die in agony
(As 'twas his fate)
No light, no love,

And all alone,
His family thrown
Out from their home -
He saw his loved ones
Cold and sad
And times for them
Gone worse to bad,
His wife weeping
'Til she died -
The children lost
And by her side.
In his mind
His anger grew,
And everything
'Gainst the rock
He threw,
His weight moved it
But not enough
For the rock was huge
And the rope was tough.
He looked up
Through the sea
To heaven,
Through the darkness
To the light
And asked that

If he died,
It might
Help his family
And see they should
Never want
For daily food,
Find happiness and love
In life's full pleasures
And love their father
Who'd loved his treasures,
Loved them 'til
His heart did burst,
And now it seemed
That he was cursed
Never to see
Those dear, dear faces
Which occupied
Such little spaces.
Salty tears began
To fill his mask,
So he pushed it up
And chok'd and gasped,
As the tears
Flowed into the deep
And his eyes slowly closed
To go to sleep.

The cottage clock
Chimed its note
And then the mother
Softly spoke
To her children, four.
"Well, my dears,
There's nothing more,
Off to bed,
Today is - Christmas
So say a prayer
To those who miss us,
Your father will
Be here I know
If it's meant to be,
So - we'll see."

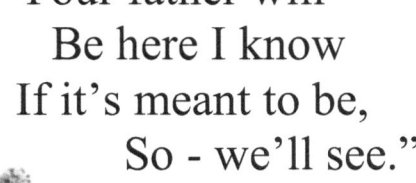

The children left
With heavy feet
To their beds
To try and sleep.

Having put Little One
Up in the loft
On her bed
So sweet and soft,

The mother went down
On her bed to lie,
But all she could do
Was to weep and cry.

Now, Little One
Lay in her
Snug bed sack
And wondered when
Her father'd be back.
She didn't believe
That he was dead,
As all the rest
Of them had said.
She lifted herself
Out of bed
And opened the window
To breathe the air,
As she did nightly
Foul or fair.
She felt the moonshine
On her face
And imagined the stars
All over the place
Flashing as her father

Would always say
Like jewels in Paradise
For those who pray.
Then she put
Her hands together
And asked that
If God might,
Or, if God could
Send her father
Home to them, safe
And never leave,
(No never again)
Then the day
Would be
Christmas indeed
(And no presents or
Food would they need)
She wished the world then
Could be as happy as they
On that wonderful
Christmas Day.
As she said this
And as she blew
Her prayer to heaven
And off it flew,

Into her hands
There softly fell
Something gentle -
And all seemed well.
She couldn't see
The white Snowflake
Fall like a star
From way up far,
She couldn't see
As her hands it touched
And around her body
A white light couched
Her tiny frame
In heavenly light
As though an angel
Of the night.
But through her darkness
She saw a stream -
A 'golden' stream
As she had dreamed,
And on its golden
Starry path
A figure stood
So happy and so good.

His arms were wide
With presents galore
For all the family
And many more
And then she heard him
Knock their door.
Little One always
Believing the best,
Jumped from the bed
With innocent zest
And ran down the stairs
With footing so sure,
And then lifted the latch
On the front door.
As it creaked
Slowly open wide,
She saw Father Christmas
Right outside, waiting
In a red-white suit
Silent as though
He were mute,
Looking unsure
As to what to do,
'Til with open arms
To him she flew,
And held him tight

With all her might
As though he were
A dream come true.
But then he
Suddenly disappeared,
And there instead -
Her 'father' appeared,
Looking at her
With such surprise,
For now he saw
She had blue eyes.
The prettiest blue eyes
He'd seen on another
(Except o'course
Those of her mother).

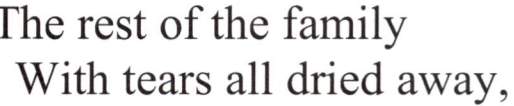

The rest of the family
With tears all dried away,
Came to see
What was at play
So early on
That Christmas Day,
And when they saw
Their father there,
And Little One

With 'happy eyes,'
Showing herself
No surprise,
They knew that there
A miracle had been
Whilst they had slept
And had not seen.

"He came," she said
On the *golden stream* -
I know I saw it,
It wasn't a dream."

Now, remember she had wished
Happiness to all,
So over the world
Happiness *did* fall -

Mr. Gold
Became so happy
That he became
A 'generous' chappy -

Smedley - Smooth
Kept her maid,
And on that day
Some tickets she paid
For 'em both to travel
To foreign climes,
As a couple of friends
Til the end of time -

Mr. Thin became
Rather round,
While Ms. Plain
Became rather vain
For she'd been turned
Into a pretty dame -

Mr. and Mrs. Ha Pi Fat
Concerned for their son
La Zi Fat
Changed his name
To, *Goo' Old Fat,*
And do you know
That was that -
For from that moment
'Til the day they died
He took such care of them,
With such deep pride.

So, all and everyone
On that day
Received some happiness
In their way
From the wish
Of that magical flake,
-

That fell from heaven
For a little girl's sake.

For more books by Robin Langford, go to:

A Story Company Publishing

www.astorycompanypublishing.com

www.ingramcontent.com/pod-product-compliance
Lightning Source LLC
Chambersburg PA
CBHW041542240626
47164CB00002B/95